One Saturday morning, I told Clifford we were going to visit
my grandma.

I brushed Clifford and put his best collar on him.

Clifford looked for his favorite toy to take along.

He couldn't find his rubber mouse, Mr. Squeaky,

anywhere around the house.

He must have left Mr. Squeaky someplace else.

Clifford didn't want to go to Grandma's house without his mouse.
I told him we would go back to all the places we went last week
to look for Mr. Squeaky.

First, we went back to the playground.

Clifford looked in the sandbox.

He searched the magic castle.

No Mr. Squeaky.

SUNDAY	MONDAY	TUESDAY	WEDNESDAY	THURSDAY	FRIDAY	SATURDAY
Play-ground	Farmer's Market	Fun Land	Uncle Bob's Farm	Family Y	Town Dock	Grandma's House

Next we went to the Farmer's Market.
Clifford thought Mr. Squeaky might be hiding
in the cabbages. But he wasn't.

FLOWERS

FLOWERS

CABBAGE 50¢

Clifford looked through the
oranges and onions.

The onions made him cry.

"Don't cry, Clifford," I said.

"We'll find Mr. Squeaky."

SUNDAY	MONDAY	TUESDAY	WEDNESDAY	THURSDAY	FRIDAY	SATURDAY
Play-ground	Farmer's Market	Fun Land	Uncle Bob's Farm	Family Y	Town Dock	Grandma's House

Fun Land was the next place we went.

Was Mr. Squeaky in the roller coaster? No.

Clifford looked in the house of mirrors...

...and the duck pond game.

No mouse there, but the man gave us a nice prize.

SUNDAY	MONDAY	TUESDAY	**WEDNESDAY**	THURSDAY	FRIDAY	SATURDAY
Play-ground	Farmer's Market	Fun Land	Uncle Bob's Farm	Family Y	Town Dock	Grandma's House

On Wednesday, we went to my uncle's farm.

Did Clifford leave his rubber mouse there?

There were mice in the barn, but none of them was Mr. Squeaky.

Mr. Squeaky wasn't in the chicken coop, either.

SUNDAY	MONDAY	TUESDAY	WEDNESDAY	**THURSDAY**	FRIDAY	SATURDAY
Play-ground	Farmer's Market	Fun Land	Uncle Bob's Farm	Family Y	Town Dock	Grandma's House

Next we went to the Family Y.

Clifford didn't find Mr. Squeaky in the gym.

He didn't see his mouse in the exercise room...

. . . or in the garden.

Where, oh where could he be?

SUNDAY	MONDAY	TUESDAY	WEDNESDAY	THURSDAY	**FRIDAY**	SATURDAY
Play-ground	Farmer's Market	Fun Land	Uncle Bob's Farm	Family Y	Town Dock	Grandma's House

We were running out of places to look.

Maybe Clifford had left Mr. Squeaky at the town dock.

Clifford looked through the boats.

Clifford looked *under* all the boats.

No rubber mouse!

We went home feeling very sad.

Dad had a surprise for Clifford—a brand-new rubber mouse!
It was a nice mouse, but it wasn't Mr. Squeaky.

SUNDAY	MONDAY	TUESDAY	WEDNESDAY	THURSDAY	FRIDAY	SATURDAY
Play-ground	Farmer's Market	Fun Land	Uncle Bob's Farm	Family Y	Town Dock	Grandma's House

On the way to Grandma's, we stopped to watch
Dad play golf. Clifford thought he had found
where Mr. Squeaky was hiding!

He was wrong.

Poor Clifford. He thought that Mr. Squeaky
was gone for good.

Grandma asked why Clifford looked so sad.

I told her about Mr. Squeaky.

She said, "Is this Mr. Squeaky? You left him here last Sunday."

"I knew we would find him!" I said.

Clifford thanked Grandma.

So did I. My grandma is the best!